THE LOST
WORLD

CONVOL
THE COLD-
BLOODED
BRUTE

With special thanks to Michael Ford

For my little brothers Kodie and Phoenix –
both proper little monsters!
Love from Big Sister Regan

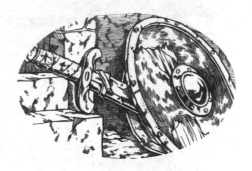

www.beastquest.co.uk

ORCHARD BOOKS
338 Euston Road, London NW1 3BH
Orchard Books Australia
Level 17/207 Kent St, Sydney, NSW 2000

A Paperback Original
First published in Great Britain in 2010

Beast Quest is a registered trademark of Beast Quest Limited
Series created by Working Partners Limited, London

Text © Beast Quest Limited 2010
Cover and inside illustrations by Steve Sims © Orchard Books 2010

A CIP catalogue record for this book is available from
the British Library.

ISBN 978 1 40830 729 8

Printed and bound in China by Imago

The paper and board used in this paperback are natural recyclable
products made from wood grown in sustainable forests. The
manufacturing processes conform to the environmental regulations of
the country of origin.

Orchard Books is a division of Hachette Children's Books,
an Hachette UK company

www.hachette.co.uk

CONVOL
THE COLD-BLOODED BRUTE

BY ADAM BLADE

ORCHARD BOOKS

Greetings, friends of the Quest...

It's been a long journey home for Tom and Elenna, after their adventures in Gwildor and Kayonia. They have left those worlds behind them now.

But if my son thought his Quests were over, he was wrong.

Adventure and peril are still ahead of Tom. Six new, terrifying Beasts must be rescued... And an enemy he thought was long gone is about to make his return.

One question remains: are you brave enough to join Tom on the most deadly Quest yet? Only you know the answer...

Freya, Mistress of the Beasts

PROLOGUE

Dalaton puffed across to the far side of the courtyard where, near a rack of fearsome looking spears, stood two of his fellow guards.

"Looks like Dalaton the Swift is in a hurry!" one said.

"He's as quick as a hare fleeing a fox," laughed the other.

Dalaton waddled past, ignoring them. He wished his stomach was slightly less rotund, but he was used to the teasing. Some said a

three-legged tortoise would beat him
in a race!

He glanced over his shoulder and
checked that the guards had turned
back to their duties. Then he slipped
away from prying eyes down a dark
passage, unlit by torches.

You shouldn't be doing this, he
told himself. *You should mind your
own business. Go to bed!* But he kept
on walking.

At the end of the passage, he
pressed himself up against a wall. He
tried to catch his breath, listening
for any sounds. There was nothing,
except for the distant neighing of a
horse in the castle stables.

If I'm caught here, he thought,
*the king will surely put me in chains.
Or worse...*

Dalaton shuddered. There was no

going back now. He peered out from his hiding place towards the steps leading down to the dungeon. The Good Wizard Oradu was being held captive there, and Dalaton wanted to help him.

But how? he thought. *What can I do?*

He crept to the top of the steps. A low moan drifted up, echoing off the dripping stone walls; perhaps he was too late... The other guards said the king was trying to steal Oradu's powers. Word was that Oradu's spellbook, cauldron and falcon had already been taken away from him.

Dalaton's skin prickled with fear as he descended the steps. His mind screamed at him to turn back, but something forced him to carry on. If he was locked down there in the dank cells, he'd want someone to come to his aid, as well.

A dim light flickered from below. Dalaton peered around the rough wall; he had to stifle the gasp in his throat.

Oradu's wrists, ankles and neck were shackled with iron manacles. The other end of the chain was bolted to the cell wall. Dalaton had seen him dragged into the castle the day before, still proud and dignified. Now his robes were streaked with dirt, and his head hung limply. They'd taken his pointed hat, revealing his grey hair, which was matted with sweat and grime.

Two guards stood in front of him. One held the wizard's staff. "Not so powerful without this, are you?" he taunted.

Oradu didn't answer. Dalaton

thought the poor man was near
the end.

"There's just the robe to go," said
the other guard. He tore it from the
wizard's body, leaving him shivering

in an under-tunic.

Dalaton shook his head sadly. *I'm too late. Now they'll finish him.*

The guard threw the robe aside and pulled a scroll from his belt. He unrolled it. Dalaton saw the wizard straighten up. There was a faint gleam in his eye. The guard read:

"By the order of the king, we hereby confiscate all of your magic..."

Whoosh!

Cold wind blasted through the chamber, catching the scroll and flinging it to the floor. Spokes of blinding light burst from the wizard's cell. Dalaton shielded his eyes and the guards cried out.

Just as suddenly, the light faded.

"Where's he gone?" shouted one of the guards in surprise.

Dalaton couldn't believe his eyes:

the chains which had held Oradu captive hung loosely from the walls. The guards stood, dumbfounded.

Oradu had disappeared!

"The king will be furious," said the other guard fearfully. "What shall we do?"

Dalaton didn't wait to find out. He tiptoed back up the stairs. A ball of dread was building in the pit of his stomach. Now that the good wizard Oradu had abandoned them, there was nothing to stop the king's evil.

Unless a new hero could be found, the kingdom was surely doomed.

CHAPTER ONE

A TWISTED KINGDOM

The portal shimmered around them,
bathing everything in a blue glow.
Wind blasted through Tom's clothes
as Avantia drew closer. He glanced
round and saw his mother, Freya,
locks of her hair whipping into her
face. Elenna was grinning as she
braced herself against the streams
of air. Marc's robes flapped against
his skinny legs. Silver panted in

excitement while Storm tossed his mane and flicked his tail. But Tom was worried.

As they sped through the magical tunnel, King Hugo's castle flickered in and out of view. On the ramparts, flying at full mast, was a black flag. A flag Tom didn't recognise.

What has been happening since I left? Tom wondered, a shiver shooting through him.

He pushed the worry away and concentrated on staying upright in the pulsing currents. Kayonia was behind them and Velmal was defeated. Soon they would be home, his father Taladon waiting for them. His family would be reunited at last!

The blue glow faded, and he saw long grass rise up towards him. Tom's feet slammed onto the ground, and as he bent his knees to cushion the blow, his body went rolling over and over. He heard Elenna cry out as she tumbled down beside him.

Tom stretched his legs, making sure nothing was broken, and climbed gingerly to his feet. Elenna was picking bits of grass off her clothes. She laughed as Silver howled happily and leapt into the air.

"That's right, boy," she told her wolf. "We're home!"

Marc staggered to his feet, straightening his robes. He gazed around, eyes wide. They were standing in a meadow, full of beautiful flowers. Storm bent his head happily and tore up a tuft of fresh, juicy grass.

Freya smiled. "It's been so long since I was in this kingdom," she said.

"We're not far from King Hugo's palace," Tom realised. "It's just over that low rise ahead."

"Let's go!" said Elenna.

They set off. Once they reached the top of the hill, King Hugo's castle came fully into view. On his last Quest, Tom had wondered if he'd ever see the battlements again. His heart swelled with joy, despite the black flag whipped by the breeze.

As they came closer, Tom noticed other changes. Many more soldiers than normal stood on the battlements, with weapons poised. From the slits in the towers, he felt a hundred arrows tracking their every move. Anxiety gnawed at him.

"It's as if they're on alert for something," said Freya.

Elenna's eyes darted from window to window, her face serious. "Could the kingdom be at war?"

"I don't know," said Tom, sharing an anxious look with Marc. The apprentice's knuckles had turned white as they gripped his staff, and his face seemed to reflect Tom's own thoughts: *something is very wrong in Avantia.*

The drawbridge was pulled up. It creaked open slowly like a giant set of jaws. The castle moat, which Tom remembered as being crystal clear, was dark and murky.

"I hope Taladon's all right," Tom said.

A trio of guards gripping sharp spears marched out. They wore uniforms of black, with gold trim and silver helmets that revealed only the gleam of their eyes through the slits.

"Who trespasses on the king's land?" bellowed one. "Speak quickly, or never speak again!"

Tom held up his hands to show they meant no harm.

"We're friends of Avantia," he said. "We've come back through a portal from another land."

The soldiers looked at each other.

"All travellers must report to the king," said one.

Tom pulled his shoulders back. "Please tell the king that Tom and Elenna are here," he said. "We have returned from Kayonia and wish to speak with him."

The lead soldier lowered the vicious point of his spear.

"First hand over your weapons," he said.

Tom didn't like it, but he began to unhook his shield from his shoulder. Elenna looked at him in alarm and gave a tiny shake of her head.

"We have to do what they say," he told her.

He unlooped his sword from his belt too. He hated being parted from it, but losing his shield was even worse. It held the six magical tokens from his first ever Quest in Avantia, which bestow him with powers over the Good Beasts. Elenna handed over her bow and arrows, muttering that she'd better get them back, and Freya held out her gleaming bronze sword with the engraved hilt. Marc raised his hands to show that all he had was his staff.

The soldier nodded gruffly. "Very well, follow me."

With a soldier on either side, they were escorted into the castle. This was not the welcome Tom had been expecting.

Inside, the air was cold and dank. Patches of moss spread over the walls. The great chain for lowering the drawbridge was covered in rust.

"It wasn't like this when I was last here," said Freya.

"Nor I," Tom agreed. The sooner he found Taladon and King Hugo, the better.

Soldiers were standing at attention in every doorway, their eyes narrowed with suspicion.

They left Storm and Silver with an attendant, and climbed the tower to the throne room.

Tom saw that the portraits of King Hugo's ancestors no longer hung on the walls. Perhaps they were being cleaned or repainted...

The great doors to the king's chamber were closed.

Strange, thought Tom. *They were always kept open before.*

The soldier used the butt of his spear to give three loud knocks.

"Enter!" called an angry, impatient voice through the door.

The doors creaked open. Inside, a huge fire blazed in the hearth. The light from the flames cast the room in long, flickering shadows.

King Hugo's throne was at the far end, and sat on it was a hooded figure.

That isn't King Hugo, Tom thought.

"Who dares disturb my peace?" said the figure.

They took a few more steps into

the room, and the firelight caught the
figure's sneering face.

Elenna gasped. "It can't be..."

Tom's words seemed locked in his
throat, but he managed to utter one.

"Malvel!"

CHAPTER TWO

KING OF TAVANIA

The Dark Wizard leaned forward and
clapped his bony hands together.
Beneath his dark hood, Malvel's pale
features twisted into a smile.

"What a pleasant surprise," said
Malvel.

"No…" Tom breathed. "This can't
be… We defeated you…"

Malvel ignored Tom. He narrowed
his eyes at Marc. "You wear a

wizard's clothes, boy!"

"I'm just an apprentice," said Marc, stepping backwards.

Malvel stood up. "Then it must be your magic that's bringing havoc to Tavania." He glanced towards the two soldiers, as if watching to see how they'd react. One whispered to his comrade.

"So it's the boy's fault!"

Tavania? thought Tom.

"What havoc?" asked Freya angrily.

She stepped forward and grasped Malvel's thin arm. He hissed with displeasure and tried to pull away, but she already had a hand around his throat. Eyes bulging, he cried out to the soldiers.

"Get this girl off me!" His voice came out high and thin. In a flash, the soldiers were at her side, peeling her fingers away from Malvel's neck and cruelly twisting her arms up behind her back. She grimaced, but went still. Tom stepped forward to intervenc, but one of the soldiers turned and pointed his sword at his throat. Tom backed off, swallowing his anger.

Malvel snortcd, rubbing his neck. "You mean you don't know?" he said at last. "You haven't seen the tears in the sky?"

He flung a hand towards the window and Tom rushed over. Sure enough, the sky here wasn't like that in his homeland. He hadn't noticed it before because of the clouds, but the whole kingdom seemed to be covered in a transparent glass dome. Strange shadows flitted across the sky, and patches of darkness opened up like gaping mouths, then snapped closed again. *We're a long way from Avantia,* Tom realised.

He turned on the Evil Wizard. "Where have you brought us?"

One of the soldiers stepped forward and kicked Tom in the back of his knees. He fell to the ground with a cry.

"Leave him alone!" shouted Elenna. Tom saw Freya writhing again in the soldiers' strong grasp.

"No one speaks to the king with such disrespect!" said the soldier who'd kicked him. Then he addressed Malvel. "They spoke of arriving through a portal, sire."

"As I suspected," said Malvel, slowly circling Tom. "It must be their fault. They are to blame for the Beasts!"

Tom's ears pricked up. "Beasts?" he and his mother said at once.

A sneer split Malvel's face. "You have brought this curse upon us."

"What curse?" asked Marc.

Malvel cocked his head towards the window. "The curse that rips Beasts from their natural homes, casting them where they don't belong. The curse that drives them mad with rage and wreaks havoc across my kingdom."

Freya had pulled free of the soldiers and came forward to help Tom up.

"This land must have a Good Wizard," said Marc. "What have you done with him?"

Malvel's eyes went cold. He raised an arm straight into the air. In his palm a red glow formed like a burning ember. Tom noticed the

soldiers moving away from Marc, as if scared.

"There's only room for one wizard in Tavania!" Malvel shouted.

He thrust his hand forward, firing out a red beam of light that struck Marc in the chest. Tom's friend uttered no sound, but his eyes went wide and he fell to his knees, his mouth open in silent agony. Elenna screamed in horror.

"Malvel, what are you doing?" shouted Tom.

He rushed towards Marc, but an orb of pink light spread out from the apprentice's body. Tom bounced off its surface and fell back. *It's some sort of shield,* he thought.

He looked desperately at Malvel, but the Evil Wizard was smiling. His fingers twitched and curled,

and white shreds of mist seemed
to emerge from Marc's body. They
threaded back along the red beam
and into Malvel's arm. Tom's friend
was shaking as though his very life
was being sucked away.

Malvel's stealing his magic! Tom
realised. He got to his feet and threw
himself against the pink bubble again,
but it was no use. It was solid as a
brick wall.

Malvel clenched his fist and the glow vanished, leaving a smell of smoke in the air. Marc teetered for a second on his knees, then limply pitched forward. Elenna rushed to his side. She leaned over his body to feel for a pulse in his throat. She looked at Tom, shaking her head.

"He's dead..." she breathed.

Tom could see that Marc wasn't breathing. Anger and pain burned through him. He tried to leap at Malvel but strong arms seized him from behind and suddenly there was a sword at his throat.

He tried to control the emotion in his voice and directed his words at the sneering wizard.

"While there's blood in my veins, I'll..."

"Yes, yes," said Malvel, waving his

hand dismissively. "You said that to me in Avantia. Goodbye!"

He clapped his hands. Tom thought that Malvel was summoning more soldiers, but instead the room around him blurred. Malvel became double; then there were four of him, wobbling in front of his throne. Tom felt sick and dizzy. With a white flash, the feel of the cold steel vanished from his neck and his feet seemed to be hovering just above the ground. Cold air tickled his skin. He was falling...

He fell against the ground and his ankle twisted beneath him. He heard Elenna grunt as she landed. Tom lay face-down, smelling damp and decay. Through the gloom he saw a set of iron bars.

They were trapped!

CHAPTER THREE

A FAMILIAR FACE

"Where are we?" whispered Elenna.

"We're in a dungeon," Tom said. He stood, testing his weight on his ankle. It would be fine. Freya was helping Elenna to her feet.

Through the iron bars a shaft of light picked out the tears on Elenna's cheeks. Tom swallowed his grief.

"We have to be strong," he said. "Marc wouldn't want us to give up."

She nodded. Tom heard a neighing outside. Storm!

He jumped up and ran to the window. Through the thick bars he saw a stable opposite. Over the half-open door his stallion poked his nose. Silver, with a rope around his neck, was tied to a post.

"Don't worry!" Tom called, his voice echoing off the slimy walls.

"We'll get out somehow."

Storm whinnied at the sound of his master.

"What have we got here?" said a gruff voice.

Tom jumped back from the grate and saw a fat prison guard coming down the stone steps into the dungeon. He was carrying a torch of burning rushes, and a ring of keys rattled around his middle. Freya watched him, her head cocked to one side, eyes narrowed.

The guard put his nose between the bars, his ample belly straining against the iron rails.

"We've done nothing wrong," said Elenna. "Let us out. Malvel's killed our friend and cast us into these dungeons. We don't belong here!"

The guard held up his hands

apologetically. "There's no doubting Malvel is a strict king," he said, "but if I was to release you, he'd have my head." Tom saw the guard's hands trembling. "Who are you?"

"I'm Tom," he said. "And this is Freya and Elenna." He pointed to his mother and friend. Elenna paced the cell angrily, and Freya still eyed the guard with suspicion.

"Well, I'm Dalaton," said the guard. "And if you're no trouble to me, then I'll return the courtesy. No more racket, understand?"

He waddled off up the stairs.

"What is this place?" said Elenna. "It looks a lot like Avantia, but everything's twisted and changed. Where's King Hugo? And Aduro?"

"I don't think they exist here," said Tom. "You saw the confusion on the guards' faces. They'd never even heard of them!"

"I've been told that portal travel can be dangerous," said Freya. "If too many are opened, the harmony of the worlds may be disrupted. Strange things can happen..."

"And now Avantia is called Tavania!" said Elenna.

"That's just it," said Tom. "I don't think this is Avantia. This is another realm entirely."

Guilt and anger twisted in Tom's stomach, making him feel sick. *Did I cause this?* he asked himself. *I went through portals from Gwildor to Kayonia, then from Kayonia to here...*

Tom braced himself against the cell bars and tried to prise them apart. He pulled until he thought his tendons would tear. But it was no good. Freya put a hand on Tom's shoulders, and he fell back, sweating.

"Don't worry, my son," she said, dull light glinting off her armour. Despite the stinking hay at their feet, she still looked like a Mistress of the Beasts. Could Tom be as brave and noble as her? "We're going to put this right," she went on.

"How?" Tom asked.

"Every kingdom needs a hero," she said, "including Tavania."

Freya was right; he couldn't give up.

"First we need to get out of here!" said Elenna.

The strewn hay started to swirl, as if a sudden draught had blown into the cell. A tall, blurred figure shimmered into life.

Tom looked about for a weapon, but there was nothing to hand.

The figure became clear. It was a man, hovering a finger's width above the ground. From the long white beard, he looked a little like Aduro, but he wore no pointed wizard's hat, or cloak. Instead, this person was dressed in simple clothes, with a tunic that came down just above his knees. His feet were bare and dirty.

"Who are you?" asked Tom.

"I am Oradu," said the man. "Good Wizard of Tavania, and advisor to the exiled King Henri."

The wizard crossed the cell. It looked as though he was going to walk straight into the bars, but instead he passed through them.

"You're not really here!" Tom gasped. He remembered what Malvel had said: "There's only room for one wizard in Tavania."

Oradu nodded gravely. "It's only your mother's belief in you that has brought me here," he said. He looked over their shoulders quickly. "I don't have much time."

"Where are your clothes?" asked Elenna.

"Malvel has stripped my powers away," said Oradu, "including my magical robes. And while the portals remain open, Malvel can feed off their dark energy. Until they are closed, neither I nor the king will be strong enough to return to Tavania."

Tom remembered Marc's powers being sucked from him. The same thing must have happened to Oradu, but at least he'd escaped with his life.

"What can we do?" he asked.

"You came here through a mystical portal," said Oradu. "This has upset the balance of the kingdom, and now six new Beasts have been cast into places they do not belong. They are lost, confused and very, very dangerous."

Tom looked at Elenna. Her face showed the same sadness he felt. He turned back to Oradu. "I'm sorry we caused this."

Oradu smiled. "A true hero dwells not on his mistakes, but vows to put them right. Only you can send the Beasts back to their natural homes and stop the chaos in Tavania."

"And if I can't?" said Tom.

Oradu's face looked suddenly grave.

"Then the portals will tear Tavania apart...if the Beasts don't do it first."

Tom straightened his shoulders and looked at his mother and Elenna.

"I won't let that happen," he said.

"I drove Malvel out of my own kingdom – I won't let him destroy this one."

Oradu's image flickered, and he smiled. "I can tell your heart is strong. I will help you when I can. With each Beast you save, one of my six items will be returned. When all six are restored, I will be at full strength. Then we can fight Mal—"

Tom gasped as he heard the scuffing of steps from outside the cell.

"What's all the noise down there?" called a voice.

Dalaton stomped heavily down the stone stairway with his torch. In his other hand was a half-gnawed chicken drumstick. He came up to the bars and peered inside. With a panicked look, Elenna scurried forwards to distract him.

But when Tom turned around, Oradu had vanished.

"Some of us are trying to rest," Dalaton went on. He took a bite of the chicken and chewed noisily.

Elenna leant right against the bars, smiling brightly. "Sorry," she said, "we were just…trying to keep our spirits up."

What's she up to? Tom wondered. *Oradu's gone. She doesn't have to cover any more.*

Dalaton wiped the grease from his mouth with the back of a grubby sleeve and shuffled off back up the stairs. Elenna turned to the others, still smiling. From behind her back she drew a ring of keys, and rattled them.

"Dalaton really isn't a very good prison guard. I managed to take these right off his belt."

"Elenna!" Tom cried. "I didn't see you do that."

"I didn't have you down as a thief," Freya said, grinning.

Elenna reached around the bars and slid the biggest key into the lock. There was a satisfying clunk as she turned the key and the door opened.

Tom felt a thrill of excitement – a new Quest was under way!

CHAPTER FOUR

ESCAPE FROM THE DUNGEON

"Where to now?" asked Elenna as they walked out of the cell and up the stone steps.

Tom stopped at the top of the stairs, peering around the corner to see Dalaton slumped on a stool with his back against the wall. He was snoring. Beside him, leaning against the wall, were a sword and shield. The shield had a torn leather covering, and the sword was rusted

at the hilt. They probably wouldn't
last long in a battle with a Beast, but
they'd have to do for now.

Tom put his finger to his lips and
they slipped past the prison guard.
Dalaton smacked his lips in his sleep
and muttered something. Tom froze,
and waited for the guard to start
snoring again. Then he picked up the
weapons. Freya was glancing at the
guard too. She gave a half smile.

Outside, Silver stood up when

he saw them approaching, but he seemed to know not to make a noise. Elenna untied the cord around his neck, while Tom unbolted the stable door. Storm swished his tail gratefully.

Now we just have to get out of the castle, Tom thought.

A track led from the stable to the drawbridge, but there were soldiers stationed on either side. They would have to distract them. The winding mechanism, with the rusty chain, was above the guard-post. Tom pointed it out to Elenna.

"If we can knock the winch off its axis, the drawbridge should open. You and Freya mount Storm and get ready – I'll do the rest."

Elenna nodded, then frowned. "Where *is* Freya?"

Tom glanced round. His mother was hanging back. He went over to her.

"It's time to leave," he hissed.

But she shook her head. "No. You and Elenna must go on alone."

"What?" Tom whispered. "I'm not leaving you here."

Freya looked at Tom very seriously. "Your Quest is to help Tavania's Beasts find their way home," she said. "Mine is to help the kingdom in another way."

"But..." Tom was so confused, he could barely speak. "I don't..."

"Tavania is a realm in chaos," said Freya, looking back to the snoring guard. "And it needs its own Master of the Beasts."

Tom followed her gaze to the portly man. "Him?" he said. "He's not a

Master of the Beasts. He's just a lazy, fat guard!"

Freya shook her head. "My instincts tell me that this might be Tavania's champion. He's just not had the chance to walk the hero's road, until now." Freya turned to him, resting one hand on the hilt of her sword, the other on Tom's shoulder. "Tom, I'm going to stay here, and see if I can help Dalaton become the champion Tavania deserves. Can you trust me to do that?"

"But...I've only just found you," said Tom.

"I know, my son. But I'll be waiting here for you at Quest's end. I promise."

"I'll come back," Tom managed to say, though his throat felt suddenly thick.

Dalaton started in his sleep and Tom held his breath. But the guard scratched his nose without opening his eyes.

"I know you can do it," said Freya. "Good luck, Tom!"

He left her side without looking back. He went over to where Elenna sat astride Storm. There was a mallet leaning up alongside the stable, and he hefted it over his shoulder. He'd need something to let down the drawbridge.

"Ready?" he said to Elenna.

"Is Freya not coming?" she asked.

Tom shook his head. "She has her own Quest," he said. "Wait here."

Tom kept to the shadows as he climbed a set of narrow stone steps up to the battlements above the drawbridge. There was a narrow passage where defending soldiers could look out over the moat, but for now it was unguarded.

Tom moved into position above the winch. The chain coiled around it was as thick as his wrist.

He lifted the mallet over his head. *If this doesn't work, we're in trouble,* he thought.

With all his strength, he brought the mallet down on the winch. It broke with a loud crack and the chain snapped free. With a grinding squeal the drawbridge crashed open. Below he could hear the guards suddenly become alert.

"What's going on?" shouted one.

"Intruder at the drawbridge!" yelled another.

Over their voices came the thunder of hooves. Tom's friends were

racing to join him. Silver was in
the lead, streaking through the gate
with Elenna galloping after him on
Storm. As the stallion burst onto
the drawbridge, the soldiers ran out,
levelling their crossbows.

"You! Stop!" one yelled.

Tom jumped off the battlements.
He landed heavily on top of the
soldiers, flooring them. He snatched

one crossbow away, and kicked the other into the moat. Then he ran after his friends, just managing to draw level with Storm, who slowed down to let him jump into the saddle behind Elenna.

"Go!" he shouted.

Elenna dug in her heels and Storm galloped across the fields. Tom took a last look at the towers of the castle. Had he done the right thing by leaving Freya?

Next time I'm here, he promised himself, *Tavania will be free from Malvel's rule.*

CHAPTER FIVE

A HIDDEN ENEMY

When the castle was no longer in sight, Elenna reined Storm to a halt, and they dismounted to check their bearings. Above them, the sky's dome reflected thousands of stars. Even the constellations looked the same as Avantia. Tom told Elenna all about Freya's decision to stay behind.

"You'll miss her, won't you?" she said gently.

Tom nodded. "But her Quest is to train Dalaton to face his destiny. She's sure of it."

"But where are we supposed to go?" asked Elenna. "We don't even know what the first Beast is!"

"We'll figure it out," Tom told her. "We always do. Let's..."

He fell silent, feeling Elenna sit bolt upright in the saddle in front of him. Both of them heard a curious low drone, somewhere behind them. Tom's hand went to the hilt of his sword – was danger near?

But when he turned his head, the first thing he saw was a curious, dull golden glow emanating from Storm's saddlebag. Tom leant back to unfasten it and reach inside. His hand closed on something like a small book. But it was cold, like metal.

He pulled it out carefully, and gasped. It was a panel of bright gold, as big as his palm, with a clasp on one side. He pushed the clasp, and with a soft click, the panel opened. But it didn't stop there. It opened again, three more times, unfolding until he needed both hands to hold it. On the surface was etched a land, which looked like Avantia.

"It's a map!" said Elenna, her eyes wide in astonishment.

Tom smiled. "Oradu must have used the last of his magic to give it to us," he said.

In the north, there were mountains and icy plains; in the south, a river; in the east, a volcano. Even the palace was marked, and a village where Errinel used to be. But here, in Tavania, the names of places were different. Tom's eyes were drawn to the bottom of the map, where one of the portals was marked, swirling like a tornado in the sky. Instead of the Ruby Desert he remembered from Avantia, here was a place called the Scarlet Sands. A name appeared in golden letters beside the portal: Convol.

"Malvel said that Beasts were falling through the portals," said Elenna. "Convol must be the first we have to face. I wonder what sort of Beast it is."

"There's only one way to find out," Tom replied, glancing over his shoulder back towards the castle they had escaped. "Let's go...before Malvel sends every soldier he has out looking for us."

Tom pushed Storm hard as they steered a wide circle away from the castle. He marvelled at how similar everything was – on the map, where Avantia had the Winding River, Tavania had the Southern River. But even if the lie of the land was the same, a look upwards reminded him that this place wasn't home. The glass dome cast an eerie light, reflecting the clouds in the sky.

When they reached the river banks, there wasn't a bridge in sight. Tom searched for and found a narrow crossing place.

"We should stop for a drink," he said. "If the Scarlet Sands are anything like Avantia's Ruby Desert, it'll be hot, and dry as a bone."

Silver lapped at the river, and Storm lowered his head to drink, too. Tom rubbed the grime from his face.

"I'd kill for a hot bath," laughed Elenna, splashing him.

"Me too," he agreed.

Tom scooped up water, trying to rinse the worst of the dirt from his hair. He scrubbed behind his ears.

Storm neighed. Tom looked back to see his stallion backing away from the bank.

"What's the matter, boy?"

Elenna gasped. "Tom, the river..."

He looked back and saw the water

bubbling like it was boiling. Two snakes of water darted out and wrapped around Tom's chest.

More watery tentacles shot out from the river. One coiled around his neck, and he felt it squeeze. Another slipped around an ankle with a soaking grip.

"Help me!" he choked.

Elenna rushed to his side, and tried to pull the arm of water from his neck, but her fingers simply passed through the rippling stream.

Another column of water leapt from the stream and enclosed her waist. She cried out and Tom watched helplessly as she was yanked into the water, her voice suddenly muffled. Silver ran to the edge of the river, howling for his mistress. Storm continued to back away, as choppy waves climbed the bank towards him. The water surged and Elenna was snatched away in the fast current.

"No!" Tom cried. He reached out a hand, but his friend was already too far downstream.

Stars spun in Tom's vision, and he knew he was close to blacking out. He stopped trying to fight the water, and instead drew his borrowed sword. He plunged it into the watery arm. The limb slid back, and Tom fell onto his knees, only just managing to keep his face out of the swirling water. Then a giant fist formed among the waves, ready to pound him. Tom rolled aside as the balled hand smashed into the bank.

Elenna was already twenty paces away, with Silver tracking her along the bank, howling in panic. Elenna flailed as the water carried her downstream. This was Malvel's work, he was sure.

If I don't get to her soon, Tom thought, *she'll drown.*

CHAPTER SIX

A TRAIL OF DESTRUCTION

Tom seized Storm's bridle to calm the panicking stallion.

"I need you now," he said, hoisting himself up. He dug in his heels. Storm responded, and charged down the bank, his hooves churning up clumps of soggy earth.

Elenna's hands were snatching at the air as the current dragged her. Ahead, Tom could see sharp rocks jutting out of the water.

As Storm drew closer to Elenna,
Tom unhooked his shield with one
hand. He stood up in his stirrups.
Elenna's head broke the surface and
she took a spluttering breath.

"Elenna!" he shouted. "Catch!"

She turned her panicked eyes to
him, and Tom threw the shield so
that it span through the air, landing
in the churning rapids just ahead of
her. She reached out and her fingers
closed on the wood.

Coughing and spluttering, Elenna thrashed her feet for all she was worth. Soon, she had heaved her body out of the current to calmer waters, swimming shakily to where Tom had drawn Storm to a stop.

"Thank you!" she called out.

Tom drove Storm further on, then jumped down and scrambled to the bank. Silver arrived beside him.

"This way!" Tom shouted, holding out his hands.

When Elenna was close enough, Tom's fingers closed on hers and he tugged. A whirlpool seemed to follow her and kept her gripped. Her lips were blue from the freezing water. Tom pulled as hard as he could, but the magic clutching her was strong. Silver fastened his teeth on her sleeve as well. Finally, with a mighty tug,

Tom and the wolf managed to drag her out onto the muddy bank.

Weak, but still afraid, she crawled up and away from the water. Tom sank down beside her.

"That was close!" she gasped. Her teeth chattered and she hugged herself. She looked nervously at the water. "What was that? It seemed like the river was alive!"

"It's Malvel," said Tom grimly. "His magic has turned the land against us."

They'd need to be on their guard; there were more than just Beasts to contend with in Tavania.

Tom glanced up at the sky, with the glittering map laid out on the ground in front of them. Night was drawing in, but he didn't want to stop.

"We should keep going," he said. "If we can get to the Scarlet Sands before dawn, perhaps we can fight the Beast while the air is still cool."

Elenna nodded. They wrung the water from their clothes and used their rolled up blankets to pat themselves dry. Silver shook himself, droplets flying from his thick fur.

Tom folded the map and they climbed into the saddle. "The sooner we get away from this river, the better," Elenna said, shivering.

They rode through the darkness across empty fields, until they felt a warm breeze blowing from the south. Fine grains of sand flew through the air, stinging their cheeks.

We must be close, thought Tom.

There were no stars, but the moon lit the landscape. Storm picked his way with difficulty around tufts of long grass among the dunes. Silver found it easier going.

They didn't see another creature; it felt as if the place had been abandoned.

"Look!" said Elenna.

Tom steered Storm in the direction she was pointing and saw a cactus with the head shorn off. There were four deep pale gouges in its flesh, as if it had been raked with claws.

"The Beast's been here," Tom murmured, staring hard at the claw marks. Clearly Convol had thick skin if he wasn't bothered by the cactus's long spikes.

Tom drove on Storm and they continued towards the desert. They found a rotting animal carcass. Its stomach was torn open and flies buzzed around. Tom pulled his tunic up over his nose to block stench.

"It's some sort of mule," said Elenna, doing the same.

Tom felt sick. The dead creature bore the same four-pronged marks on its neck, except these ones were caked with blood. He steered Storm away. "We need to find Convol before he hurts any other animals – or people," he said.

Soon he spotted something ahead. He slowed Storm to a walk. As they came closer, Tom saw dozens of dome-shaped, single-storey buildings dotted around a central square.

"It's a settlement," said Elenna.

Tom nodded. "Perhaps there are people who can direct us to Convol."

But as they stepped among the clutch of buildings, things did not look good. Tom saw two upturned market carts between the houses. The canvas awnings had been slashed – four vicious tears in each. There wasn't a person in sight.

"Convol's been here," said Elenna.

Tom swallowed. Did that mean all the people had met the same fate as the camel they'd found?

There was a noise behind him, and a stone the size of his fist landed on the ground. Tom turned in the saddle, his hand reaching for the hilt of his sword. A second stone arced through the air, and smacked into Storm's flank. The stallion snorted and bucked, and Tom could do nothing as he was thrown from the saddle with Elenna. Silver pawed the dust, howling defiantly.

Tom landed with a thump, but regained his feet quickly. Turning, he eyed the gaps between the houses, looking for danger. Elenna sprung up, too, crossbow levelled.

From the dark doorway of a house, Tom spotted the white glint of eyes. Someone – or something – was watching them.

Tom unsheathed his sword, aiming the point towards the stranger.

"Show yourself!" he challenged.

CHAPTER SEVEN

A DESERT MONSTER

A small boy crept out. From his thin limbs and sunken cheeks, Tom guessed he was starving. His lips were dry and cracked.

"Sorry about your horse," said the boy, looking about nervously. Then his eyes fell on Tom's sword. "Are you some sort of knight? Are you here to fight the monster?"

Monster? It could only be one thing.

Tom lowered his weapon and Elenna did the same.

"Tell us what you've seen. What does this monster look like?"

"I've seen something," replied the boy, casting another anxious glance around into the darkness. "A monster like a lizard. But the biggest lizard I've ever seen in the Scarlet Sands. Must be thirty paces long, with teeth the size of your hand. It attacked our village."

"And where are the other villagers?" asked Elenna.

Tears began to well up in the boy's eyes, silver in the moonlight. "We needed water," he said. "But the only place is a nearby oasis. The Beast guards it. The others have gone into the desert to find another source." He paused, wiping away a tear. "I don't know if they'll come back."

Tom put his arm around the boy's shoulders. "Don't worry," he said. "We're here now."

"Will you make the monster go away?" asked the boy.

"I'll do my best," said Tom. "Which way is this oasis?"

The boy pointed behind the houses. Tom couldn't see anything in the gloom. "There are three large dunes that look like pyramids. The oasis is behind the middle one."

"That's where we'll go," said Tom.

The boy's face brightened. "Wait!" he said, scurrying back indoors.

Tom took a few steps closer to the house. There was a little yard in front, but the plants that had once grown there were parched and brown. Elsewhere the ground was torn up as if cattle had stampeded through.

"This Beast has to be stopped," he said to Elenna.

The boy came running back out of his house, with two cloaks. "It gets hot in the desert," he said. "These will keep you cool."

Tom felt a rush of gratitude. This might be a strange new kingdom, but that didn't mean its people were not kind-hearted. The boy looked uncertainly at Elenna as she donned her cloak. "Are you going to fight the monster, too? You're only a girl."

Elenna frowned and folded her arms, but Tom smiled. "She's the bravest person I know," he said.

"Well, good luck," said the boy. "You'll need her bravery this time, I think."

They left the boy one of their water flasks, and walked out of the village as the first rays of dawn broke over the horizon, their cloaks wrapped around them. Tom saw the great expanse of desert stretching out ahead. The temperature rose with the sun, and the horizon became a shimmering blur. Tom had to shield his eyes and squint to see where he was going. Elenna pointed through the heat haze at three large dunes, side by side.

"That must be the place the boy was talking about," she said. "Make for the middle dune."

Tom adjusted Storm's course to scale the plateau. Storm struggled up the shifting dune, and Silver panted. Tom and Elenna shared the last few drops from their water flask.

"We need to find more soon," Tom said. "Otherwise we'll die of thirst."

They reached the top of the dune. Over the rim, the desert stretched as far as the eye could see. A short way off was the oasis the villager had spoken of. It was an island of green in the sea of golden sand.

The open portal hovered above, like an angry gaping mouth in the dome of the sky.

"One good thing about the desert," said Elenna, "It'll be hard for Convol to sneak up on us."

But where is the Beast? thought Tom. *It must be hiding in the oasis.*

Tom steered Storm in zigzags down
the side of the dune, and towards the
lush oasis. He could already see the
clear water, and Storm started to trot,
eager for a drink.

They reached the water's edge and
Storm lowered his head to drink
deeply. Silver lapped beside him. The
surface was as still as a mirror.

"What if Malvel controls the water
here, too?" asked Elenna.

Tom was looking anxiously around,

expecting to see Convol charging over the sand.

"Let's just fill our flask and find somewhere to wait," he said.

The heat of the desert blasted him as he bent over the water. He wondered how long they'd even last out here...

A small wave rippled across the oasis, lapping at the bank.

Tom's head snapped up. He couldn't see anything in the lake. But something must have caused the movement.

"Elenna..." he said.

First one spike, then a row, punctured the surface of the water. Then came a tail, covered in vicious spikes. Now a green-brown body, thick-skinned and studded with warts, emerged. Tom drew Storm

away from the bank as the head of
the Beast reared up.

Tom gripped his shield, but it
felt hopelessly small against such a
huge foe, whose long snout opened
wide in a roar that shook the plants
around them.

The first Beast of Tavania had
arrived!

CHAPTER EIGHT

THE COLD-BLOODED BRUTE

Convol lunged through the water, lashing his tail like a whip towards them. It thudded into Storm's legs, sweeping them from under him. The stallion whinnied in pain and Tom and Elenna crashed on to the hard desert ground.

Dizzily, Tom managed to get to his feet as Storm twisted upright. He drew his sword, but it felt awkward, different from his old one. He reminded himself that the amber jewel in his belt, won from Tusk the mighty mammoth, would sharpen his skills.

Elenna clambered to her feet and tugged him back from the water towards the sand.

Silver continued to growl, but even he backed off. Convol lumbered out onto the bank after them. He had four legs, each ending in fearsome yellow claws.

Convol twitched his muscular body and his great tail arced over his back like a scorpion's sting. Tom only just managed to raise his shield in time. The tail crunched onto the shield, knocking Tom to the ground and jarring his shoulder.

Convol roared and swung his tail again. Tom deflected the bone-rattling blow – but only just. The Beast let out an angry bellow, revealing rows of rotten teeth in the glistening green gums. They looked capable of tearing flesh to pieces. Sour breath carried over the air towards Tom.

Elenna, riding on Storm, appeared between him and the Beast. Storm's hooves threw up sand as she pulled him to a stop. Silver stood bravely by the stallion's side.

"Over here!" she called.

Convol's red eyes lit up and he twisted to face the new threat. He swung his tail at Elenna but she managed to swerve the stallion aside. Silver darted forwards and tried to snap at the Beast's snout, but was driven back by a raking claw.

"Get away!" shouted Tom.

Elenna didn't move straight away. She waited until Convol came after her, lumbering completely out of the water. *She's distracting him,* Tom realised. At the last minute, his friend dug in her heels and Storm's hooves sprayed a clot of sand into Convol's gaping jaws. She trotted away, with Silver following. The Beast was enraged, his eyes flickering behind double lids as he watched Elenna.

What's that? Tom noticed that Convol's spiky back no longer glistened. The water was drying up in the sun, leaving patches caked with sand. The Beast's thick hide was starting to look stretched and tight, almost as if it was shrinking with the lack of water. *Convol isn't meant to be in the desert,* Tom remembered. Of course! This Beast wasn't invincible, after all. Darting forwards, Tom slashed at Convol's hide. But his attack was clumsy and the blade glanced off the skin.

Convol suddenly gave a strange high-pitched noise between a snarl and a hiss. The sound seemed to slice

through Tom's head and he clutched his hands to his ears. He didn't see the tail swinging through the air until it was too late.

It caught him in the stomach and tossed him through the air, sending his cloak flapping. Tom thumped into the sand. His body lurched with pain and he struggled to catch a breath. As he shook his head clear, he saw the Beast charging after Elenna.

She was managing to keep ahead of the Beast, but it was surprising how quickly Convol propelled himself across the dunes with his stocky, powerful legs. The Beast snapped and snarled at Storm's hooves, but the stallion managed to pull away again, just in time.

Now the sun was directly overhead, glaring down on them. The cracks forming over the Beast's tight and shrunken skin looked as though they were driving him mad with frustration. He lunged through the sand as he pursued Elenna, and his cries of anger were tinged with pain. *He needs water as much as we do*, Tom thought.

Tom ran across the dune, calling to Elenna: "Bring him back this way!"

But the cloak kept getting caught beneath his feet, and he tripped and stumbled on the uneven ground. Sweat and sand stung his eyes.

We need to end this soon, he thought.

Elenna hadn't heard him shout. She'd set Storm at a gallop back towards the water. Silver darted ahead of the stallion.

"No!" shouted Tom. "Not that way!" The water was the only place the Beast could survive in the desert.

But Elenna careered onwards, straight for the oasis. Convol was only a horse-length behind, drooling into the sand and thrusting himself onwards. A sudden breeze caught up a flurry of sand. As it swirled around Tom, he felt sure he could hear Malvel's wicked laughter in his ears.

You'll fail, Tom, echoed a voice.

When the air finally cleared, Tom saw something that made the blood drain from his cheeks. Convol's deadly tail was raised in the air above Elenna and Storm. One swipe of that fearsome weapon and his friends would be killed.

CHAPTER NINE

THE BEAST FIGHTS BACK

As Convol threw himself forwards, Elenna yanked on Storm's reins and the stallion veered aside, splashing in the shallows. Convol couldn't stop though; the weight of his bulk was too great. In a blur of bulging muscles, writhing tail and flashing claws, the Beast tumbled into the oasis. A great curtain of water rose up into the air.

Above them, the portal's fringes rippled, scattering sparks of every colour. Tom could see it was somehow connected with the Beast. If that portal had brought Convol here, it must be his way home, too.

"Quickly!" he shouted. "Get behind me."

Elenna brought Storm around and Silver followed. Convol was on his belly, smashing his tail angrily into the water, driving waves to the banks, as he fought to right himself.

"It looks like we've made him really angry," she said.

"Convol hates the heat," Tom told her. "If we can get him back out in the sand, we stand a chance of defeating him."

He looked down at his wooden shield, now warped from its time in the river. His borrowed sword had nicks along the blade, and a rusty hilt. *These are the only weapons I have,* he told himself. *They'll have to do.* He couldn't allow this kingdom to be tortured like this; as long as it was in chaos, Malvel would be able to take advantage.

"We need to split up," he said to Elenna, thinking quickly. "That way we give the Beast two enemies to focus on. I can't fight him face to face. Stay here until I call you."

Tom cast off his cloak, and felt the sun start to burn his skin. But he couldn't fight in the cloak, so he had no choice. He approached the water's edge, holding his sword aloft.

"I'm ready for you now!" he shouted.

The Beast submerged for a

moment, dousing himself in water, before reappearing nearby. His outer eyelids blinked menacingly, and the great tail swayed to and fro, driving his body through the water.

Tom ran along the bank to the left, to get closer to the portal.

Convol came on through the shallows with a burst of speed, and the tail lifted from the water, showering droplets. This time Tom was ready. When the club descended, he jumped aside. It thudded into the sand, leaving a deep hollow.

Tom tucked his shield tight into his side as the Beast's claws swung at his ribs. He thought he heard the shield crack and buckle under the blow. He bashed the arm away with the flat of his sword. He backed away, to lure the Beast further out.

"Come and get me!" Tom
challenged.

The Beast dragged its huge,
glistening body onto dry land.

Elenna was edging closer on Storm.
Silver kept close to the stallion's legs,
his teeth bared, ready to attack.

The Beast darted forwards with
its snout, and Tom barely pulled his
arm out of the way before the teeth

snapped shut. He smashed his shield into Convol's nose, and the Beast shrank back, hissing in agony. Then he struck with his tail again. Tom defended the blow, but by now his shield was too weak. Upon impact, one edge broke away, driving a splinter deep into Tom's arm.

Tom gritted his teeth against the pain as he felt blood on his skin. There was no way he was dropping his shield. Without it, he was dead.

"Elenna," he yelled. "I need you to keep him busy. But be careful!"

His friend nodded and cantered Storm towards the Beast, her cloak whipping back from her shoulders. Convol saw her coming and flashed his body round to face her. Elenna wheeled around and set off along the bank, with the Beast in pursuit.

As soon as he was sure Convol was following his friend, Tom hoisted his sword over his shoulder. *I hope this works!*

He flung the sword as hard as he could. It spun towards the Beast, lodging in its tail. Convol slithered to a halt, stunned. Tom wasted no time. He ran up the Beast's tail, pulling out his sword as he went.

The body started to move, but Tom managed to keep his balance as he stumbled along Convol's thick hide, avoiding the cruel, jutting spikes.

As the Beast started to thrash around, trying to throw him off, Tom fell to his knees just behind the snout, gripping onto the hard ridges of his head. Convol's eyes swivelled in their sockets and his claws scrambled in the sand.

The Beast's massive jaw shook from side to side, snapping on air.

Tom lifted his sword hilt and brought it down hard on the Beast's snout. Convol roared. Tom brought his hilt down a second time. Convol's jaws closed weakly. Tom slammed a final time. The Beast's eyes rolled back in his head and his legs gave way with a jolt. Convol slumped in the sand.

A surge of power flooded Tom's chest. Convol's life was his for the taking. He'd won! The people of the village could get their drinking water without fear from now on. Tom jumped off, and positioned his sword over the Beast's skull.

One thrust and it would all be over...

CHAPTER TEN

AN ACT OF MERCY

Convol's eyes blinked slowly as he
looked up at Tom. The anger that
had lurked there, the look of evil and
hatred, vanished. Through the power
of the red jewel in his belt – which
he had won by defeating Torgor the
minotaur – Tom felt the Beast's fear...

And he knew he could not kill him.

Tom lowered his sword and stepped
aside. He saw that Elenna was

open-mouthed. But she wasn't looking at him – her eyes were focused upwards, into the sky. Tom looked, too.

The portal was ripping wider apart, taking up more and more of the domed sky. Tom began to panic. Had he done something wrong? Was Tavania going to be destroyed? The fringes of the portal gleamed blue, then red, then orange.

Convol roared. Tom stumbled back as wind rushed through his hair. A fraction at a time, the Beast's body lifted off the sand. It was like watching a hawk hovering in the air. Convol's tail sagged as he rose higher and higher. Tom stared up at the pale belly of the Beast.

Convol didn't seem afraid as he was lifted higher and higher. With a whoosh, the Beast was sucked through the portal, shrinking until he was just a dot. A heartbeat after he disappeared, the portal's lips closed like a healed wound.

The sky went black and the kingdom with it. It was as if the sun had been suddenly snuffed out. Then the sun blinked on again. Above, there was no sign of a portal.

"He's returned home!" Tom gasped.

Elenna climbed off Storm and rushed to him, Silver racing at her heels.

"We did it!" she said. "And you didn't have to kill the Beast!"

"I'm glad," said Tom.

Something floated down towards them.

"Is it a bird?" said Elenna, squinting with her hand over her eyes.

"I don't think so," said Tom. "It's too big."

The object drifted closer, and Tom saw it was a purple garment, marked with intricate gold patterns.

"It's a wizard's robe!" said Elenna.

The material fluttered lower. But instead of simply falling into the sand, it arranged itself over the ground into the shape of a body, as if being worn by an invisible man.

Not quite invisible, though. In the bright desert light, Tom caught the ghostly outline of someone he recognised.

"Oradu!" said Elenna.

"Greetings, Avantians!" said the wizard. "I can see that the kingdom of Tavania is in safe hands."

"But...how are you here?" asked Tom.

"I am here, and yet I am not," said Oradu. "With each Beast you send safely home, my aura will grow in power."

"Your aura?" said Elenna.

"Malvel stripped my magic from me," said Oradu sadly. "With each successful Quest, it returns."

"And if we send home all six Beasts," said Tom. "You'll be complete again?"

"That's right, Tom," said the wizard. "Only then will I have the power to challenge the Evil Wizard."

"Then we won't rest until the Quest is over," said Tom. "Malvel can't be allowed to stay on the throne."

Oradu nodded. "You will need more than just fighting spirit, young heroes. For there are five more Beasts to help. The next is a Beast of fire and rage. Are you ready?"

Tom shared a look with Elenna. She stood straighter and nodded.

"We're always ready," said Tom.

Oradu smiled. "Then I wish you good fortune."

With those words, the shadowy outline vanished and the robe collapsed in on itself, shrinking and folding neatly. It fluttered through the air like a butterfly, and Storm's saddlebag magically opened. The robe disappeared inside.

"It looks like we'll have Oradu with us all the way!" said Tom smiling.

"Look, Tom!" said Elenna.

As Tom turned, he saw they were not alone. A row of faces watched them from over the dune. Men and women in long, sand-swept cloaks. At the front was the boy from the deserted village. He waved at them, and from the village a cheer erupted.

"Come down!" shouted Tom. "It's safe again."

The men and women streamed towards the water, kicking up sand. Tom realise that whatever the hardships, his Quest was worth it.

"Come on," he said to Elenna, turning to face the desert. "We've only just started."

Here's a sneak preview of Tom's next
exciting adventure!

Meet

HELLioN
THE FIERY FOE

Only Tom can save Tavania from the
rule of the Evil Wizard Malvel...

PROLOGUE

Eldor lifted his head and sniffed
the air, feeling the breeze tickle his
vast antlers. The stag smelt nothing
unusual in his forest kingdom. His
does were safe as they grazed, with
their fawns close by. And yet...

Eldor had long been king of this
forest. It held no secrets for him. His
senses were as sharp as an eagle's
talons, and had never once let him
down. And now they were telling
him that a change was in the air.

And, in the forest, change was
never good.

Eldor leant his head back and
roared a warning to the unseen
enemy. The does looked up, flicking
their ears in alarm. Fawns sensed
their mothers' unease and pressed

closer, their soft speckled bodies
trembling. Eldor walked slowly in
the midst of his family, looking for
unfamiliar tracks on the forest floor.

Eldor's head darted up. His nostrils
flared. His body tensed. On the air,
was the scent of the thing he and his
family most feared.

Smoke.

Eldor would never forget the day
when, as a fawn, fire had ravaged
the woods. His father had perished,
as had many others – of all clans and
species. Eldor's nerves quivered as
a rabbit darted between his legs with
wide fearful eyes. In the distance,
a curl of smoke twisted among
the trees.

**Follow this Quest to the end in HELLION the
FIERY FOE.**

Win an exclusive
Beast Quest T-shirt and goody bag!

Tom has battled many fearsome Beasts and we want to know
which one is your favourite! Send us a drawing or painting of
your favourite Beast and tell us in 30 words why you think
it's the best.

Each month we will select **three** winners to receive
a Beast Quest T-shirt and goody bag!

Send your entry on a postcard to
BEAST QUEST COMPETITION
Orchard Books, 338 Euston Road, London NW1 3BH.

Australian readers should email:
childrens.books@hachette.com.au

New Zealand readers should write to:
Beast Quest Competition, 4 Whetu Place, Mairangi Bay,
Auckland NZ, or email: childrensbooks@hachette.co.nz

**Don't forget to include your name and address.
Only one entry per child.**

Good luck!

Join the Quest,
Join the Tribe

www.beastquest.co.uk

Have you checked out the Beast Quest website? It's the place to go for games, downloads, activities, sneak previews and lots of fun!

You can read all about your favourite Beasts, download free screensavers and desktop wallpapers for your computer, and even challenge your friends to a Beast Tournament.

Sign up to the newsletter at www.beastquest.co.uk to receive exclusive extra content and the opportunity to enter special members-only competitions. We'll send you up-to-date info on all the Beast Quest books, including the next exciting series which features six brand-new Beasts!

All books priced at £4.99,

special bumper editions

priced at £5.99.

Orchard Books are available from all good bookshops, or
can be ordered from our website:
www.orchardbooks.co.uk,
or telephone 01235 827702, or fax 01235 8227703.

FREE COLLECTOR CARDS INSIDE!

Series 7: THE LOST WORLD
COLLECT THEM ALL!

Can Tom save the chaotic land of Tavania from dark
Wizard Malvel's evil plans?

CONVOL
THE COLD-BLOODED BRUTE

978 1 40830 729 8

HELLION
THE FIERY FOE

978 1 40830 730 4

KRESTOR
THE CRUSHING TERROR

978 1 40830 731 1

MADARA
THE MIDNIGHT WARRIOR

978 1 40830 732 8

ELLIK
THE LIGHTNING HORROR

978 1 40830 733 5

CARNIVORA
THE WINGED SCAVENGER

978 1 40830 734 2

Series 8: The Pirate King
COMING SOON!

Balisk the Water Snake
Koron, Jaws of Death
Hecton the Body Snatcher
Torno the Hurricane Dragon
Kronus the Clawed Menace
Bloodboar the Buried Doom

Mortaxe the Skeleton Warrior controls the good Beasts of Avantia. Can Tom rescue them before it is too late?

978 1 40830 736 6

The Chronicles of Avantia

FROM THE DARK, A HERO ARISES...

Dare to enter the kingdom of Avantia.

A dark land, where wild creatures roam
and people fight tooth-and-nail to
survive another day.

And now, as the prophecies warned, a new evil
arises. Lord Derthsin – power-hungry and driven
by hatred – has ordered his armies into the
four corners of Avantia. Just one flicker
of hope remains...

If the four Beasts of Avantia can find their
Chosen Riders – and unite them into a deadly
fighting force – they might have the strength
to challenge Derthsin. But if they fail, the
land of Avantia will be lost forever...

FIRST HERO – OUT NOW!
Book two, CHASING EVIL,
out in October 2010, with more
great books to enjoy in 2011.

www.chroniclesofavantia.com